iVy + bEAN

BOOK 5

More Praise for IVY + BEAN

★ "Just right for kids moving on from beginning readers . . .
illustrations deftly capture the girls' personalities and the tale's
humor. . . . Barrows' narrative brims with sprightly dialogue."
—*Publishers Weekly*, starred review

★ "In the tradition of Betsy and Tacy, Ginnie and Genevra, come
two new friends, Ivy and Bean. . . . The deliciousness is in the
details here. . . . Will make readers giggle."
—*Booklist*, starred review

"A charming new series." —*People*

"Ivy and Bean are a terrific buddy combo." —*Chicago Tribune*

"Readers will be snickering in glee over Ivy and Bean's antics."
—*Kirkus Reviews*

"This is a great chapter book for students who have recently
crossed the independent reader bridge."
—*School Library Journal*

"Annie Barrows' simple and sassy text will draw in both the
reluctant reader and the young bookworm. Fans of Beverly
Cleary's Beezus and Ramona will enjoy this cleverly written and
illustrated tale of sibling rivalry and unexpected friendship."
—*BookPage*

iVy + BEAN

BOUND TO BE BAD

BOOK 5

written by annie barrows + illustrated by sophie blackall

chronicle books · san francisco

To Sally, who is nothing at all like Nancy. —A. B.

For Sarah, Angus, and Anna, who are never, ever bad. —S. B.

This is a component of a boxed set. Not for individual retail.

Butterfinger is a registered trademark of Société des Produits Néstlé S.A.
M&M's is a registered trademark of Mars, Inc.
Milk Duds is a registered trademark of The Hershey Company.
Tootsie Roll is a registered trademark of Tootsie Roll Industries, Inc.

Book design by Sara Gillingham.
Typeset in Blockhead and Candida.
The illustrations in this book were rendered in Chinese ink.
Manufactured in China.

MIX
Paper from
responsible sources
FSC™ C020056
www.fsc.org

ISBN 978-1-4521-4223-4

The Library of Congress has catalogued the hardcover edition as follows:
Barrows, Annie.
Ivy and Bean bound to be bad / by Annie Barrows ; illustrated by Sophie Blackall.
p. cm. — (Ivy and Bean ; bk. 5)
Summary: Best friends Ivy and Bean learn that being very good, or very bad, can be a real
challenge when they set out to become so pure of heart that birds and animals follow them.
ISBN 978-0-8118-6265-3
[1. Behavior—Fiction. 2. Human–animal relationships—Fiction. 3. Neighbors—Fiction.
4. Family life—Fiction.] I. Blackall, Sophie, ill.
II. Title. III. Series.
PZ7.B27576Iwc 2008
[Fic]—dc22
2008005280

2 3 4 5 LEO 17 16 15 14 13

Chronicle Books LLC
680 Second Street, San Francisco, California 94107

www.chroniclekids.com

CONTENTS

A PAIN IN THE KAZOO

Check. Bean's mom was reading the paper.

Check. Bean's dad was reading the paper.

Check. Nancy was reading the funnies.

Bean picked up her plate and licked the streaks of leftover syrup.

"Bean's licking her plate," said Nancy.

"Stop it, Bean," said Bean's mom without even looking up from the paper.

Bean sat on her hands and stared at her plate with her lips shut tight. Then, suddenly, her tongue shot out of her mouth and her head swooped down to her plate. "I can't help it," she said, licking. "There's a magnetic force pulling my tongue out of my mouth."

Bean's family looked at her like she was a bug. An ugly bug.

"That's disgusting," said Nancy.

"Bean, please . . . " said her mother.

"Cut it out," said her father.

"I can't!" slurped Bean. "The force is too strong!"

Her father took her plate away. Bean slumped against the back of her chair. "Thanks, dude. I owe you one."

"Don't call me dude," said her dad. "Go do the dishes."

"What?! It's Nancy's turn!" yelped Bean.

"It was Nancy's turn until you licked your plate. Now it's your turn," said her dad.

"That's totally unfair!" huffed Bean. "I couldn't help it! Haven't you ever heard of forces beyond your control?"

"Yes, I have," said her father. "Forces beyond your control are going to make you do the dishes."

"What am I, Cinderbean?" Bean said. "What about my rights?"

Slowly her dad lowered his newspaper and looked at her. "Think about whether you're making a good choice or a bad choice, Bean."

There was a pause.

"I guess I'll go do the dishes." Bean clomped into the kitchen.

+ + + + + +

"Bean, you didn't see my pink yarn, did you?"

Oops. Bean tried to roll behind the couch, but Nancy saw her.

"Bean! Do you have my pink yarn?"

"No," said Bean. That was true. She didn't have it. She would never have it again.

Nancy looked at her, slitty-eyed. "Do you know where it is?"

"No." Who knew where it was by now?

Nancy's eyes got even slittier. "Have you seen it recently?"

"Recently?"

"Mom! Bean took my yarn!"

Before she knew it, Bean was having to look around her room for her money. (She changed hiding places so often that it was hard to remember where she kept it, exactly.) She had to give Nancy seven dollars to buy new yarn. Seven dollars! Now she only had two dollars and some coins left.

And the yarn hadn't even worked. Bean had fallen out of the tree anyway.

+ + + + + +

Bean's mom was under her desk. She was doing something with wires, and Bean could tell she wasn't having much fun because she kept saying, "Oh, for crying out loud!" and "Gee-Zoo Pete!"

"Hi, Mom," said Bean into the crack between the desk and the wall.

"Oh. Hi," said her mom. "Hold on to this cord a sec, will you?" She shoved a black wire up through the crack.

Bean didn't take it. "Only if you pay me."

"What?"

"Only if you pay me."

There was a silence. Then Bean's mom began to back out from under her desk.

Bean started to have a bad feeling. "Sorry," she said quickly. "I'll hold the cord for free."

But now her mom was all the way out. Now she was standing. Now she was glaring. "Did I hear

you say that you would help me only if I paid you?" she asked.

"It was a joke," said Bean. "Just kidding. Ha."

Her mom was still glaring. "What do you think I'm thinking, Bean?"

Bean sighed. "I think you're thinking I'm a pain in the kazoo."

"Right. So what might be a good thing for you to do?"

Bean thought. "Eat only bread and water for a week?"

"Try again," said her mom.

"Give you and Daddy and Nancy each a big wet kiss?"

Her mother coughed. "Maybe later. Try again."

"Go outside and play?"

"Bingo."

TOUGH COOKIES

Bean flopped down on her front steps. Yikes. Even though it was still morning, the wood was already hot from the sun. Bean's head was sweating under her hair. She wished she hadn't popped her blow-up pool. Her mom had said that jumping around a blow-up swimming pool on a pogo stick would pop it. Bean had said it wouldn't. Her mom had been right. Bean had been wrong.

Bean rested her chin in her hands and thought about that. She had popped her blow-up pool. She had been a disgusting bug at breakfast. She had used up Nancy's yarn. And she had made her mom mad. What if I *am* a pain in the kazoo, she thought. What if that's just how I *am*? What if I'm worse than all the other people in the world?

Bean jumped up. She wanted to play with someone. Right this minute. She looked around Pancake Court. Mostly everyone was still in-side, but there was one kid out. It was Katy, who was six years old and lived at the other end of Pancake Court. She was walking along, pushing a little pink doll stroller in front of her.

"Hiya, Katy," called Bean. "You want to play?"

Katy stopped in front of Bean's house. She looked at Bean. "I don't think so."

"Why not?" asked Bean.

"I have to stay clean." Katy was very clean. Her pink dress was clean, and even her white sandals were clean.

"How come?" Bean asked.

"We're going out for dinner tonight," said Katy.

"Your mom's making you wear your fancy stuff all day?" Bean's mom would never try that.

"She's not making me," said Katy. "I like this dress because then we're twins." She pointed to her doll.

It was true. The doll and Katy were wearing the same pink dress.

Bean felt big and dirty. "We could play a clean game."

Katy thought for a minute. "House?"

Bean hated House. "What about Starving Orphans?"

Katy folded her arms. "House."

Boy, Katy was a tough cookie. "Fine. House."

Katy was the mother. Her doll was the older sister. Bean was the baby. Katy was making cookies. The doll was doing her homework. "Now you eat the cookie dough, and I give you a time-out," said Katy to Bean.

Fine. Bean lunged toward Katy and snatched her imaginary bowl of dough.

"Gimme that!" she hollered and threw herself under the camellia bush to gobble it up.

"Oh, you're a bad girl!" scolded Katy. "You get a time-out!"

"Now I'm barfing on your shoes because I ate all that cookie dough," said Bean, crawling toward Katy.

"Eew, no!" squealed Katy, jumping away.

"Okay," said Bean. "I'm barfing on my sister's homework."

Katy grabbed the doll. "That's gross, Bean. I don't want to play that."

"Okay, let's say I have to go to the hospital and get my stomach pumped." Bean made a sound like a siren.

Katy looked down at Bean. "No," she said firmly. "You're not doing any of that. You're in a time-out."

Bean looked up at Katy. This game was too much like life. When she and Ivy played House, the house burned down. Bean wished she were playing with Ivy. "All right. I'm in a time-out. See you later." She got up and started toward the sidewalk.

"Where are you going?" asked Katy.

"Ivy's. My time-out is at Ivy's," said Bean. "Bye."

BIRD BRAINS

"IIIII-VEEE!" Bean shouted into Ivy's mail slot. "Yoooooo-hooo!"

"Hello, Bean," said Ivy's mom, opening the front door. "Care for a slice of cucumber?" She was holding a plate of them.

Bean wanted to say, Are you nuts? But she knew that wasn't polite. "No thank you," she said. "Is Ivy home?"

"She's out in the yard," said Ivy's mom. "Go on back."

Bean walked down the path beside Ivy's house and opened the gate that led to the backyard. Ivy's yard didn't have a trampoline like Bean's, but it did have big rocks and a perfectly round puddle that Ivy called a pond even though she had to fill it with the hose. Ivy was standing still in the middle of the long, weedy grass. Her arms were raised to the sky, and she had a big smile on her face.

"Are you trying to fly?" called Bean.

Ivy turned to Bean and smiled even bigger, but she didn't move. "Hi," she whispered.

"Wave your arms," advised Bean.

Ivy smiled so hard her eyeballs bulged out.

"What the heck are you doing?" Bean asked.

"I'm trying to be good," whispered Ivy.

"What?" yelled Bean. She waded through the weedy grass.

"I'm trying to be good," Ivy whispered again.

"Why do you have to be so quiet about it?" Now Bean was whispering, too.

"Because I don't want to scare the birds away. I'm trying to be so good that birds land on my fingers and wolves come out of the woods and follow me down the street," Ivy explained.

Bean stared. "Why would being good make birds land on your fingers and wolves do whatever you just said?"

"I found out about it yesterday. If you're super-good and pure of heart, animals think you're one of them and they love you and follow you around."

Ivy's arms were trembling. She must have been holding them up for a while. "Are you sure about this?" asked Bean.

"Positive. I saw it in a picture. There was this guy with birds flying all around him and a wolf licking his foot. My mom said this guy was so good that wild beasts talked to him and birds swarmed after him."

"I don't get it. *Why* did the birds swarm after him?"

"Because his heart was so pure and kind that they saw that he was the same as an animal on the inside. They loved him," Ivy said.

Bean thought about that. "Like Snow White, you mean?" Hadn't the birds helped Snow White make a pie?

Ivy made a face. "Snow White wasn't good. She was a goonball. Everyone knows you're not supposed to eat stuff you get from strangers."

"But the birds liked her," said Bean.

"Maybe the birds felt sorry for her, but they didn't think she was one of them," said Ivy. "Anyway, I don't want to be like Snow White. I want to be like the guy in the picture. I want a wolf to follow me because I'm pure of heart."

A wolf. Bean pictured a shaggy wolf walking beside her while a bird rested on her shoulder. Her mom and dad would be scared half to death, but Bean would say, "The wolf won't hurt you. He's my friend." Then the

wolf and Bean would give each other long, understanding looks. And then Bean's mom and dad would feel rotten because they hadn't realized that Bean was so pure of heart. They had thought she was a pain. Bean smiled at Ivy. "A wolf would be pretty cool."

"Yeah." Ivy smiled dreamily.

"We could share him," said Bean.

"Sure we could," said Ivy. "That's what good people do. They share."

"He doesn't even have to lick my foot," said Bean. "It's fine if he just follows me around."

"I know," said Ivy. "Me, too." She raised her arms again. "But I'm starting with birds. I think they'll be easier to get than a wolf. You know," she whispered, "they're not so smart." She looked up and smiled at the sky. "La-la-la," she sang sweetly.

"I don't see any birds," said Bean, glancing up.

"Me neither," said Ivy. "Maybe they're hiding in the trees."

Bean watched her for another moment. "I like birds, too," she said in a loud voice. "Almost as much as wolves." She held her hands upward. "How do you do it?"

"What?"

"Be so good that a bird lands on you?"

"You can't think about yourself. You have to think nice thoughts about other people," said Ivy.

Bean concentrated. She thought, I love you, Mom. I love you, Dad. Even though you're totally unfair. She thought of Nancy. Oh, I guess I love you, too, Nancy. Then she thought of Nancy saying, "Seven-year-olds aren't allowed to go to horse camp, so HA!"

and "Isn't it past Bean's bedtime, Mom?" Stupid Nancy, I hope you fall off a horse. Oops.

"Boy, this is harder than it looks," she said to Ivy. "I can think nice thoughts about my mom and dad, but that's it."

"Oh, your mom and dad are too easy. You aren't good enough if you just think nice thoughts about your mom and dad. You have to think nice thoughts about mean people."

"Holy moly, I can't even think nice thoughts about Nancy, and she's my sister."

"I'm thinking nice thoughts about Crummy Matt," Ivy announced.

"No way!" said Bean.

Crummy Matt was the meanest kid Bean knew. He was so mean he told little kids that chocolate milk was brown because it had poop in it. He was so mean that he kicked kickballs onto the school roof on purpose, so no one else could play with them. He was so mean he threw rocks at cats.

"Uh-huh," said Ivy proudly. "I am."

"There's nothing nice to think about Crummy Matt," said Bean.

"I'm thinking that I hope he stops being so crummy," said Ivy. "Hey—it's working!"

A little brown bird was hopping near Ivy's pond. Boing, boing, boing.

Ivy held her breath.

"Here, birdie!" squeaked Bean.

The bird flew away.

Ivy sighed. "Now I have to start all over again."

"Sorry," said Bean.

Ivy smiled in a pure-of-heart way at Bean. "Now I'm thinking nice thoughts about *you*," she said.

Bean didn't like the sound of that.

A CRUMMY PLAN

Bean could not think one more nice thought. She had thought something nice about every single kid in her class. She had wished that there were peace on earth and no more litter—that should make the animals happy— and that everyone had plenty to eat and only things they liked.

Not one bird had come anywhere near her.

There was sweat dripping out from under her hair.

Plus, her arms ached.

"Shoot," said Bean, dropping her arms. "How long was it before the wolf licked that guy's feet and followed him home?"

Ivy dropped her arms, too. "I think it only took him a few minutes, but we're just beginners. He was an expert. The mayor called him out especially to talk to the wolf because the wolf had been eating up the townspeople. In the picture, there were all these arms and legs lying around. But the good guy and the wolf had a talk, and next thing you know the wolf licks his foot and only eats vegetables."

"Arms and legs lying around?" asked Bean. Gross. But interesting.

"Yeah," said Ivy. "He was a really bad wolf until he met that good guy."

Bean pictured herself patting the wolf's shaggy head. He was trotting alongside her with his wolf claws clicking on the sidewalk. Grateful townspeople waved. "I bet the people were pretty glad not to be eaten, too," she said.

"Hey," said Ivy. She was smiling—a real smile, not a thinking-nice-thoughts smile. "What if we did something like that?"

"What? Put fake arms and legs around?" Bean asked.

"Not that," said Ivy. "I mean turning evil to good. If we turned a bad person into a good person, it would be almost like getting a wolf to stop eating people."

"Yeah," said Bean. "That would mean we were so good that we could infect other people with our goodness." She could almost feel the goodness oozing out of her. "That's a great idea. Who should we gooden up? Nancy?"

"No," said Ivy firmly. "Crummy Matt."

Bean stared at Ivy. "Are you bonkers? He's going to squash us like bugs." Crummy Matt was ten years old. He

bragged that when he was three, his mother had taken him to the doctor because she was worried he was a giant. The doctor said that Crummy Matt wasn't a giant. He was just big. Crummy Matt said he was the biggest ten-year-old in the country. He said there was a bigger ten-year-old in China, and that was the only reason why he wasn't the biggest ten-year-old in the world.

"No, he won't," Ivy said, "because we're going to change him into a good person."

"How are we going to do that?"

Ivy looked around as if she would find the answer in the grass. "I don't know," she said after a moment. "Maybe just looking at us will make him nice. That's what happened with the wolf."

Neither of them moved.

"We probably need a snack first," said Ivy.

They each had some banana chips. Then Bean needed some milk. She spilled quite a lot of it. They wiped it up. Then Ivy had to go to the bathroom. Then Bean had to.

When Bean came out of the bathroom, Ivy was smiling her pure-thoughts smile. "Come on," she said through her smiling teeth. "Let's get going."

Bean nodded. They walked toward the living room. Ivy's mom was lying on the couch with cucumbers all over her face. By now Bean was so good she didn't even laugh.

"Bye, Mom," said Ivy. "I love you."

Ivy's mom lifted her head a little. A cucumber fell on the floor. "What?"

"I love you."

"Where are you going? It sounds like you're leaving forever," said Ivy's mom. More cucumbers fell off her face.

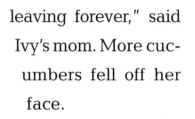

"We're going over to Matt's," said Ivy.

"You are? I thought you didn't like him," said Ivy's mom.

"Sure I like him," said Ivy. "I love everybody."

"You do?" Ivy's mom sounded surprised.

"Yes I do," said Ivy.

"It's no good saying it inside," Bean pointed out. "The birds can't hear you."

"Birds?" said Ivy's mom. "What birds?"

"We might have a bunch of birds coming to visit," explained Ivy.

"And something else, too," said Bean. "Something with lots of teeth. But don't worry."

Ivy's mom looked from Bean to Ivy. "Worry? Me? Never." She picked up her cucumbers and put them back on her face.

A GOOD BAD IDEA

 As it turned out, Ivy and Bean didn't have to go to Crummy Matt's house because Crummy Matt was already out on the sidewalk, surrounded by kids. There was his little brother, Dino, who was eight. There were Sophie W. and Sophie S. and Liana, who was Katy's older sister. Katy was sitting on a paper bag on Sophie S.'s lawn. And there was Crummy Matt's rat, Blister. Poor Blister. He wasn't very old, but he was tired anyway. He was tired because Crummy Matt was always making him do tricks.

Ivy and Bean walked toward the group. When they got closer, they heard Liana say, "Matt, that's really mean! Put him down."

"He likes it," Crummy Matt said.

"No, he doesn't," said Dino. "He hates it."

"Shut up," said Crummy Matt. "You don't know." He held Blister by the tail, dangling him over the sidewalk. Blister twisted and squeaked. He hated it.

"Boy, is he *crummy*," said Bean softly.

But Ivy was already speeding down the sidewalk. "Matt!" she cried, "Matt! Don't be cruel! Put the poor thing down!"

Crummy Matt looked up, surprised. Ivy had never talked to him before. "What?" He swung Blister a little.

Ivy clasped her hands together. "Matt, I beg you! Put him down! You're harming an innocent creature!"

The Sophies, Liana, and Katy looked hopeful. Even Blister looked hopeful. Dino didn't.

"Nobody asked for your stupid opinion," said Crummy Matt, "so shut up."

Ivy and Bean glanced at each other. It didn't seem like Ivy's goodness was doing much to Crummy Matt. In fact, it seemed like Ivy's goodness was making him mad. Bean thought maybe it was time to leave.

But Ivy took a breath. "Matt, you're a really horrible person, but you could change. If you put Blister down, I'll be your friend forever."

Bean got ready to run.

Crummy Matt carefully put Blister in his shirt pocket.

Ivy smiled purely.

Crummy Matt reached out and pulled Ivy's sparkly headband off her hair. "Who says I want to be your friend?" he said and threw the headband into the street. Then he turned around and went into his house.

+ + + + + +

Ivy was thinking loving things about all living creatures, even disgusting creatures like eyeless sea worms. Then a hummingbird whizzed past her head. It was beautiful.

Ivy pictured the shimmering creature on her shoulder like a little jewel and held her breath. Careful. Don't move. Think like a hummingbird. *"Vvvvvvvum,"* she murmured.

"What?" said Bean.

Ivy shook her head. Shhh, Bean. The hummingbird darted from flower to flower. Come on, look at me, thought Ivy. See how good I am. The hummingbird came to a stop on a stem and turned to look at her thoughtfully. For a second, Ivy was a hummingbird inside. Then—whoosh. The bird zoomed past her head again and disappeared into the blue sky.

Ivy was discouraged. The hummingbird hadn't even noticed her pure heart. Her headband was still in the street and was probably going to get run over. Bean had told the other kids about the birds and the wolf, and now Sophie W., Sophie S., Liana, and Dino were lined up on the curb across Pancake Court, staring at Ivy. Katy was there, too, sitting on her paper bag, staring. It was distracting.

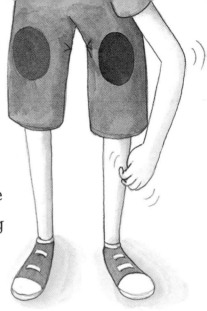

Bean was distracting, too. She was standing beside Ivy on the lawn. She was supposed to be holding up her arms for the birds, but she kept bending down to scratch her legs. No bird in its right mind was going to land on Ivy's fingers if Bean kept on scratching like that.

"Stop scratching," whispered Ivy.

"I've got mosquito bites," explained Bean. "Want to see?"

"No," said Ivy. She dropped her arms and turned to Bean. "Look, Bean, I'm sorry, but I don't think you're concentrating hard enough to get a bird."

"Hey!" Bean felt herself turning red. "I'm concentrating. I'm just itchy."

"I don't think you're thinking loving thoughts. I think you're thinking about how itchy you are."

"Hey! I can't help it if I'm itchy. And if you're so good, you should be feeling sorry for me because I'm itchy," said Bean.

"I *do* feel sorry for you," said Ivy. "But you're not supposed to feel sorry for yourself. You're not supposed to be thinking about yourself at all! You're going to ruin my chance to have birds and wolves because you're weakening my goodness."

"I am not!" yelled Bean. "I'm just as good as you are! I'm not thinking about myself! I'm thinking loving thoughts!" She glanced around Ivy's front yard and spotted a ladybug on a leaf. "See? Look at that ladybug! She wasn't there a minute ago! She's following me!" Bean kneeled down beside the leaf. She was eye

to eye with the ladybug. The ladybug froze.
Bean tipped her head like she was listening.
She nodded. "This ladybug says she can feel
how pure of heart I am."

"She does not," Ivy said.

"How do you know?" Bean yelped. "Your heart isn't so pure. That's what this ladybug here—" Bean jabbed her finger toward the leaf. "Oops." Bean had jabbed too hard and the ladybug had fallen off the leaf and dropped to the ground. "Sorry, little ladybug," whispered Bean, hurrying to turn the ladybug right side up. The ladybug scuttled away as fast as it could.

Bean thumped down on the grass. "I saved her life. That was good!"

"But you knocked her over first," Ivy said.

"Dumb bug," Bean scowled.

Ivy looked at her. "Wait a minute," she said.

"What?"

"I'm getting an idea."

"Jeez. I hope it's more fun than being good," said Bean grumpily.

"Way more fun," Ivy said.

"Well? What is it?" asked Bean.

"Being bad."

THE WORST WORD IN THE WORLD

"Let me get this straight," Bean said. "I do something bad, and then you talk me into being good?"

"Yeah," said Ivy. "I reform you. Just like that guy reformed the wolf."

"I'm not licking your feet," said Bean. "No way, no how."

"I don't want you to lick my feet," Ivy said. "I just want to make you good."

"And I'll still get to share the wolf and the birds when they come along?"

"Sure. They'll love you extra because you turned from bad to good."

Bean thought about that. "But I won't be bad in the end, right? The wolf is going to know I'm like him inside, right?"

"Right," Ivy said. "You'll only be bad for a few minutes. Then I'll reform you, and you'll be good again. It's like a play we're putting on for the birds."

"What's going on over there?" yelled Liana from the curb. "I thought you said birds were going to flutter around your head!" She pointed to the three crows who lived on the telephone pole. "I don't see them fluttering!"

"Hang on!" Ivy called.

"We're pausing for station identification,"
Bean yelled. She turned back to Ivy. "Am I
just bad once?"

"Well, that depends," said Ivy, "on how long it takes for the birds to show up."

Wow. Being bad was actually good. Bean jumped to her feet. "Okay, guys!" she yelled at the kids on the curb. "I'm going to be really bad, and then Ivy's going to make me good. Then we'll have birds galore. Not just those crow losers."

"How bad are you going to be?" yelled Dino.

"You wait and see," called Bean. "You won't believe it."

She'd better think of something quick.

She looked around Ivy's front yard.

She scratched her mosquito bites.

She searched through her brain for badness. The problem was that she usually didn't decide to be bad. For example, she knew that she wasn't supposed to call Nancy a doody head, but when she got really mad, she forgot. She didn't mean to be bad; she was just too mad to remember to be good.

Maybe she should call Ivy a doody head. But she didn't truly think Ivy was a doody head, so that probably wouldn't count.

Bean pulled a leaf off a bush and looked at Ivy. "Bad?" she asked.

Ivy shrugged. "Not really. My mom cuts them with clippers."

Okay. She would have to do something worse.

She just couldn't think of anything. "What's bad?" she asked.

"Bad words," Ivy said instantly.

Of course! Bean should have thought of that herself! Just a few days ago she had heard a lot of bad words at the hardware store. Some of them were so bad that she didn't know what they meant, so she picked the one that had sounded the worst. She turned to face the kids on the curb. "I'm about to say a bad word!" she yelled. "A super-duper bad word!"

Dino, Liana, and the Sophies nodded. Katy clapped.

Bean stood very close to Ivy and whispered the bad word in her ear.

Ivy tried not to giggle, but it came out her nose. She sniffed hard and then put her hands over her heart and cried, "NO! I beg you, Bean, not to say that terrible word! Promise you won't!"

Bean looked at Ivy for a moment. What was she supposed to do? "Um, okay."

"She's good again! She's changed!" Ivy said loudly.

Bean checked the crows. They were still sitting on the telephone pole. They hadn't even noticed Bean's bad word.

"Stupid birds," said Bean.

"We didn't hear anything!" Dino yelled.

"Say it louder!"

Whoa, Nellie. Bean was not going to say *that* word out loud. Um, um . . . "BRA!" she screamed.

Liana and the Sophies giggled, but Dino hollered, "That's not a bad word! That's boring!"

What?! Boring? Bean was insulted. She wasn't boring! She was bad! She was the worst kid in town!

She stormed out of Ivy's front yard, charged up the sidewalk, and came to a stop in front of Mrs. Trantz's house.

Bean turned her head to glare at Dino. "You want to see bad?" she yelled. "Watch this!"

BEAN, QUEEN OF BAD

In Mrs. Trantz's yard, there were two rows of rosebushes, one on either side of the front path. Each rosebush had a little circle of dirt to live in. Each circle of dirt had a tiny white fence around it and then a sea of sparkly white rocks stretching out around that. Sometimes Mrs. Trantz came outside and washed her front path. Sometimes she even washed her rocks.

Mrs. Trantz liked things to be very clean. When she saw dirt, her face shriveled into a frown. When she saw children, her eyes narrowed into tiny slivers. When she saw dirty children, her frown sucked her lips all the way inside her mouth and her eyes slivered into nothing. She frowned so hard her face went away.

Bean drove Mrs. Trantz crazy. She didn't try to; she just did. Every time Bean walked by Mrs. Trantz's house, one of the tiny white fences circling around the rosebushes fell over. Bean didn't know how it happened. Then Mrs. Trantz would call Bean's mother and say that Bean was destructive. That meant she wrecked things.

Bean didn't know quite what she was going to do to Mrs. Trantz's yard, but it wouldn't be boring, that was for sure. She stood in front of the stiff rosebushes and looked carefully to see if Mrs. Trantz was peeking from behind her curtains. The coast was clear.

"Do something!" yelled Dino. "This is boring!"

Boring! Bean would show him!

She leaned over the tiny white fence and brought her face close to a rose. And then she spit on it as hard as she could.

She turned around to face Dino. "How was that, huh? You'd never do that!"

Ivy grabbed her by the shoulders. "Bean!" she cried. "Promise you'll never do that again! You're hurting the flowers, and they have feelings, too!"

Oh. Right. Just for a second, Bean had forgotten about turning good. "Yeah, sure. I'll never do it again," she told Ivy.

"She's reformed!" yelled Ivy.

But Bean whirled around to make sure Dino was watching. "Oh no!" she hollered. "It didn't stick! I'm turning bad again!"

This time the Sophies clapped along with Katy.

Ha! Bean was the Queen of Bad! "Keep your eyes peeled!" she screeched and started to run toward her house.

Bean knew a lot of things that Nancy didn't know she knew. One of the things she knew was where Nancy hid candy. Nancy thought she was pretty smart. She didn't hide candy in her own room. She hid it in the bathroom, behind the stacks of toilet paper, in a brown paper bag. What Nancy didn't know was that Bean spent a lot of time prowling around the house, looking for treasure. One day when she was prowling in the bathroom, Bean found Nancy's paper bag full of candy.

Bean was always careful not to eat so much candy that Nancy would notice. Just a Tootsie Roll or a mini–candy bar—that's all she ever took. Until today.

Bean whisked into her house and rushed to the bathroom. Bean often rushed to the bathroom, so her mom and dad and Nancy didn't even notice. When she came out, there was a bulge inside her shirt, but nobody was watching.

Bean marched back up the street toward Ivy's house, but she didn't stop there. She walked around Pancake Court until she was standing next to Dino, Liana, the Sophies, and Katy. Ivy came running. "What are you doing, Bean?" Her eyes were shining.

"Look," said Bean. She pulled the brown paper bag from her shirt. "I've got candy. Except it isn't mine. I stole it."

"Great!" said Ivy. "Who'd you steal it from?"

"Nancy," said Bean.

Ivy giggled.

"Hey, you're supposed to be good," said Bean, and Ivy stopped giggling. "I'm going to eat stolen candy," Bean said to Dino and the other kids, "before lunch and in front of you guys, without sharing." She reached into the bag and looked at Ivy. "How's that for bad?"

Everyone watched while she ate a Butterfinger.

"Aw, come on," said Katy. "Give us some. Please?"

"No," said Bean with her mouth full. "I'm so bad I don't share with anyone. Right, Ivy?"

Ivy nodded, her eyes on the candy.

Bean opened a pack of peanut-butter cups and ate one.

"Isn't your sister going to be mad?" asked Liana.

"Yg," said Bean, jamming the other peanut-butter cup into her mouth. She was starting to feel a little sick. She looked at Ivy. "Aren't you going to stop me?" she whispered.

"Oh! Right!" Ivy said. She clasped her hands together and said, "Bean, I beg you! Stop stealing and eating dessert before lunch and not sharing! You've got to get good."

Bean was glad to stop eating candy. "Well, okay, since you put it that way."

"You should give us some to show that you're reformed," said Ivy.

Bean thought about that. "No. Because it's stolen, you'd be doing something bad if you ate it. All of you."

"I don't care if I'm bad or not," said Liana. "I want some Milk Duds."

"Halt!" said Ivy, stepping between Bean and the other kids. "I can't let you go down the path of badness by eating this candy." She smiled her pure-of-heart smile.

"Yeah," said Bean. "And right now I'm reformed so I can't lead you down the path of badness either."

"This is dumb," said Dino. "It's just a little piece of candy."

"Stolen candy," Bean reminded him. "And it's before lunch, too."

"I didn't steal it," said Dino. "And what if I want to be bad, anyway?" He reached around Ivy to grab the bag.

But someone was already there.

It was Katy.

She ripped the bag out of Bean's hands

and tore down the street, her white sandals flashing in the sun.

Bean looked at the shred of paper bag in her hands. "Wow," she said. "Badness is catching."

FROM BAD TO WORSE

They all stood there watching Katy run away. Suddenly, Dino slapped his hand against his forehead. "Oh no!" he groaned. "Now I've got it, too!" He looked sideways at Bean. "I think I've got it bad!"

Sophie W. smiled. "Me, too," she said. "I've got it worse."

"Now wait a second," began Ivy.

"I'm the bad one around here!" said Bean.

"You wish," said Liana. She glanced at the row of front yards that lined the street. "First dibs on all the mailboxes," she said.

+ + + + + +

Kids were swarming around Pancake Court.

Dino stole one of Mrs. Trantz's white rocks. Ivy begged him to stop, but he just stuck the rock in the exhaust pipe of Jake the Teenager's car.

Sophie W. ripped a bunch of grass out of her lawn.

"Stop it," Ivy pleaded, and Sophie obeyed. But a minute later she hid her baby sister's shovel and pail in a bush.

"Look at me!" Bean hollered. She took off her sneakers and tried to throw them onto Mrs. Trantz's roof. One bounced off the living room window and the other landed in the camellia bush. Bean was glad she hadn't broken the window, but she turned to Ivy and said, "Dang! I was trying to break the window."

"Bean! Breaking windows is really bad!" cried Ivy. "You can't do that! Reform!"

But Bean wasn't listening. She whirled around, looking for another bad thing to do.

+ + + + + +

Ivy dropped down on her front lawn. She had been running back and forth between badnesses, but nobody was getting any better. Dino was stepping on ants. Sophie S. was rubbing dirt into her shirt. Liana was tying her mother's hose in a knot. Bean was hanging upside down from the handrail on her front stairs. Sophie W. had swallowed her gum.

Ivy glanced up into the trees. Still no birds. Even the crows had flown away.

Bean sat down beside her. "I can't think of anything else. Can you?"

"No." Ivy looked around the yard for ideas. "Hey! A squirrel!" Ivy whispered, pointing at her hedge. "He's looking at me!"

Inside the hedge, a little brown squirrel was sitting among the leaves. He was holding a strawberry in his tiny claws. Every few moments he lifted the berry to his mouth and tore it to bits with his chattering teeth. Little pieces of strawberry flew through the air, but he paid no attention. His bulging brown eyes were fixed on Ivy.

"He's trying to tell me something with his eyes," whispered Ivy, staring at the squirrel.

Bean nodded. "Cool."

"He's saying, 'O pure one, I will follow you till the end of time because your heart is like a squirrel's.'" Ivy stood and stepped toward the squirrel. "Greetings," she whispered.

The squirrel leaped to its feet as though it had been stuck with a pin. Stuffing the rest of the berry in its mouth, it scampered away.

Ivy frowned. She turned to Bean. "I've got it. Let's pick a bunch of strawberries and squash them. That would be pretty bad."

"Great idea!" said Bean.

Dino ran by, dragging a big branch behind him. "I'm worse than you!" he hollered over his shoulder at Bean.

"We're going to touch Mr. Columbi's car!" shrieked Sophie S. and Sophie W. Mr. Columbi was always telling them not to touch his car. He washed it two times a week with special soap. The two Sophies bounded toward Mr. Columbi's driveway.

Liana was stuffing her mother's welcome mat into her mailbox.

Bean looked up and down Pancake Court. What more could she do? The strawberries were squished, her sneakers were gone, she was sick to her stomach from candy, she had spit on Mrs. Trantz's rose, and she had said the worst word in the world. She was pooped.

"These guys are ruining everything," said Ivy, watching Dino scamper by with another branch.

"Ha-ha!" he shouted. "You're just a good little girl."

"Who asked you?" yelled Bean.

"You're not even close to bad!" he yelled. "You don't even know how to be bad! You're GOOD!" Off he ran.

"You're a stinky face!" Ivy hollered after him.

Then she turned to Bean. "Come on, Bean," she urged. "Show him how bad you are."

"I have an idea," Bean said slowly.

Ivy smiled. "What is it?"

"It's not enough to be bad myself," Bean explained. "I think I have to do something bad to someone else." She looked at Dino tearing around with his branch, and then she looked back at Ivy. "Where do you keep your hose?"

BEAN OVERBOARD!

Ivy's mom had one of those long hoses on a wheel. It was attached to the side of Ivy's house. The two girls carefully unwound it from the wheel.

Ivy went around and stood in front of Dino's house. "Hey, you guys!" she called. "Bean's about to be really bad!" Dino, the Sophies, and Liana looked up from their own badness. "You'd better come here and sit down," Ivy said. "You're going to want to see this one up close."

The kids walked toward Ivy. "What's she going to do?" asked Dino.

"I can't even say it." Ivy made her eyes big. "I've begged her not to do it, but she just can't help herself," she said, shaking her head. "You should sit down on the curb and watch."

Dino and the girls exchanged glances. Then they slowly sat down on the curb in front of Dino's house.

"Is she going to drive her dad's car?" asked Liana.

"You have to wait and see," said Ivy, smiling mysteriously.

"Aw, come on," said Dino. "Is she going to blow something up?"

"Sort of," said Ivy, smiling even more mysteriously. "You guys just close your eyes for a few minutes, and then you'll see."

"Why do we have to close our eyes?" Sophie W. asked.

"It's like before the movie begins. It has to be dark for the surprise to work," Ivy said.

They looked at Ivy suspiciously.

"Come on. Just for a few minutes," said Ivy. "If Bean's going to get in all this trouble, you can at least close your eyes. I'll tell you when to open them."

Dino looked at the girls and shrugged.

"Okay," said Sophie S.

They closed their eyes. Ivy tiptoed away.

"They've got their eyes closed, but we'd better be quick," Ivy said.

Running across lawns to keep their steps silent, Ivy and Bean carried the hose from Ivy's driveway to Dino's. Luckily, Dino's faucet was in the same place as Ivy's. They screwed the hose into it, and Bean ran tiptoe down the driveway toward the row of kids on the curb. Ivy stood at the faucet, waiting.

With the hose in her hand, Bean walked quietly toward the curb until she was standing right behind Dino. "Hey Dino!" she said softly, holding her hand over the end of the hose, "You can open your eyes now."

Ivy twisted the faucet on.

Dino opened his eyes and turned around.

And Bean blasted him right in the kisser.

"AAAAAH!" he screeched, jumping up.

"Not so boring now, is it?" laughed Bean. The hose waggled in her hand.

"Hey!" roared Liana.

"Bean!" squawked Sophie W. and Sophie S.

Uh-oh. Bean hadn't meant to get them wet.

"Your turn!" yelled Liana, yanking the slippery hose from Bean's hand.

"Yeah!" screamed Sophie S.

"Get her!" hollered Dino.

Bean could hear Ivy yelling in the distance. "I beg you, Bean, stop spraying those poor, innocent children."

"I'm not spraying them," Bean hollered. "They're spraying me!" She whirled around and tried to make a break for it, but before she had taken two steps, she slammed into a giant wall.

Oops. It wasn't a wall.

It was Crummy Matt.

THE REVENGE OF DINO

"What the heck are you doing to my little brother?" Crummy Matt shouted, grabbing Bean by the shirt.

Up at the top of the driveway, Ivy turned off the water. Suddenly everything was very quiet.

"Um, nothing?" Bean asked.

Crummy Matt didn't let go of her shirt. He turned to Dino. "What did she do?"

"She made me shut my eyes, and then she sprayed me!" Dino said. He shook his head and water flew in a circle. "I'm all wet!" he yelled.

"We all got wet!" said Sophie W. "She sprayed all of us, just to be mean!"

"I wasn't being mean," Bean tried to explain. "I was being bad."

"But now she's going to be good—forever," said Ivy. She had come up behind Crummy Matt, and now she stood next to Bean. "She'll never do it again."

Crummy Matt sneered at them, first at Bean and then at Ivy. "Nobody messes with my little brother," he growled.

"Yeah," nodded Dino. "Get 'em, Matt."

Crummy Matt nodded seriously. "Okay, bro." He bent and whispered into Dino's ear.

Dino smiled and ran up the driveway.

Crummy Matt held on to Bean's shirt.

"She'll never do it again," Ivy said softly. "She's going to reform. She's sorry."

Really, Bean was only a little sorry. It had been fun seeing Dino's face right before she blasted him. But she nodded her head up and down.

Crummy Matt didn't say anything. He just held on to Bean's shirt, and soon Dino came rushing back down the driveway. In his arms, he carried a rope.

I could run away, thought Bean. I probably wouldn't even have to rip my shirt very much.

"Bean!" Ivy whispered.

"Zip it," snapped Crummy Matt. "Grab her, too," he said to Sophie W.

Sophie W. grabbed one of Ivy's arms, and Liana grabbed the other.

"Traitors," said Ivy, but she didn't say it very loud.

"Hup!" said Crummy Matt. He yanked on Bean's shirt. "March!"

They stopped in front of a big tree at the side of Crummy Matt's yard. Crummy Matt pushed Bean against the tree trunk, and Sophie W. did the same to Ivy. "Start with their feet," Crummy Matt told Dino. Dino kneeled and began wrapping the rope around Ivy's and Bean's ankles.

All at once, Ivy started singing, "Join us in the paths of goodness, and the birds and beasts will love you!"

Bean shook her head. She didn't think this was going to work.

"Reform!" sang Ivy, "and hummingbirds will flutter around your head!"

Crummy Matt didn't care about birds. "Can it!" he barked.

"I'm thinking good thoughts about you anyway, Matt!" sang Ivy.

"Well, stop it," said Matt.

"Time to be good," sang Bean half-heartedly, "La-la-la."

"Tie them tighter," ordered Crummy Matt. Dino squeezed the rope around Ivy's and Bean's waists and arms. Round and round he went, with the Sophies and Liana helping. Crummy Matt watched.

"I know this great knot," Dino said. "They'll never get out." He worked busily on the other side of Bean. "Done," he said, standing up.

To heck with wolves and birds, Bean thought. She was tired of being bad. At least before, she had only been bad by mistake. I'll just be normal, she decided, and she stuck out her tongue at Dino. "This is boring."

"Oh yeah?" said Dino. He smiled wickedly. And then he picked up the hose.

GOOD AND SOGGY

Bean was drenched. Her hair was sticking to the sides of her face, and water was dribbling out of her shorts pocket and down her legs. She wiggled her legs against the rope. It didn't move.

The only part of Ivy that wasn't wet was the top of her head. "My shoes are squishy," she said.

"It feels kind of good," said Bean. "I got sweaty being bad."

She watched Crummy Matt holding the
hose, spraying it high into the air so that water
came down like rain. Dino, Sophie S., Sophie
W., and Liana were stamping in the mud
puddle at the end of the driveway.

It looked like a lot of fun.

"Come on," called Bean. "Let us out!"

"Never," said Crummy Matt. "You got to stay there forever!"

"Maybe the birds will rescue us," said Ivy, but not like she believed it.

Bean heard a little voice. "Hi, Bean."

It was Katy. She was peeking around the side of the tree. "I'm sorry I ate all your candy."

"Oh, that's okay," Bean said. "It wasn't my candy anyway."

Katy stepped around in front of Bean. The front of her pink dress was smeared with chocolate. "I got all messed up," she said.

"Yeah," said Bean. "Are you in trouble?"

"Not yet," said Katy. "I don't care anyway." There was a pause. "Are you going to be bad some more? That was better than House."

"I'm sort of stuck here," said Bean. "Unless—hey, Katy, will you push that rope up a little? The one on my knee."

Katy pushed the rope up, and Bean felt the knot under her fingers. "This is not such a great knot," she said.

Katy was looking at the kids in the mud. "I'm already dirty," she said thoughtfully. "A little more won't make any difference." She ran down the lawn toward the puddle.

The knot was getting looser.

Suddenly Crummy Matt came running up to the tree. "Here," he said to Ivy, pulling Blister out of his pocket. "You got a rat on your head." He put Blister on the top of Ivy's head. "If you move, he'll chew your hair off." Then he ran away, back to his hose.

"Yuck," said Bean. Rats gave her the creeps.

Ivy felt Blister's little feet scrabbling against her scalp. His stomach rested, fat and warm, on her hair. She could hear the squeaky sound of his breath inside her head. "Is he eating my hair?" she asked Bean.

Bean strained to see the top of Ivy's head. "Hang on a sec," she said. She pulled the rope until the free end slid out of the knot. All at once, the rope sagged. She had done it! "Ta-da!"

Now she could see. She stood on tiptoe and looked. Blister, dry and comfortable at last, stretched across Ivy's head. "No. He's sleeping," said Bean. "I'll get him off." She reached up.

"No!" whispered Ivy. "Leave him there!"

"Really? You don't mind?" asked Bean.

"No! Don't you get it?" whispered Ivy. "He's an animal, and he's following me! Because I'm pure of heart!"

Bean stood on tiptoe again. Blister did look happy. So did Ivy. "How long are you going to let him stay there?" she asked.

"He can stay forever if he wants to," said Ivy firmly. She stood very straight so Blister wouldn't fall off.

Bean glanced at the mud puddle. Now Katy was stamping in it, too. "I'm going to stop being bad. I'm just going to be regular."

"That's okay," said Ivy. "I've got Blister. You can be regular now."

"Okay," said Bean. She turned around and ran down the driveway toward the mud puddle. "YAH!" she screamed, jumping into the center.

Big drops of mud flew through the air, spattering over Dino, the Sophies, Liana, and Katy.

"Get her!" yelled Liana, but Bean darted away and grabbed the hose from Crummy Matt. Before he could blink, she had sprayed him in the face. Then she whirled around and around, water spurting in a circle. Nobody could get near her.

"You'll never take me alive!" she yelled.

Crummy Matt jumped at her and slipped sideways down the grass. Liana was chasing Katy. Dino and Sophie S. were laughing so hard they were choking. Sophie W. was scooping big handfuls of mud and throwing them at Bean.

But up by the tree, Ivy and Blister rested peacefully, both pure of heart.

IVY + BEAN QUIZ!

HOW WELL DO YOU REALLY KNOW IVY AND BEAN?

Come one, come all! Test your Ivy and Bean knowledge! Earn a star for every correct answer! And don't worry—peeking at the answer key is fine!

1. What fruit does Bean smash into Leo's hair?

    (Hint: *Ivy and Bean and the Ghost That Had to Go,* **BOOK ❷**)

    a. bananas

    b. spiders

    c. plums

    d. kumquats

2. What is the name of the dog that lives on Pancake Court?

    (Hint: *Ivy and Bean,* **BOOK ❶**)

    a. Hester

b. Hippolyte

c. Bob

d. Fester

3. The world's record for Number of Spoons on the Face is . . .

(Hint: *Ivy and Bean Break the Fossil Record*, BOOK ❸)

a. 4

b. 15

c. 42

d. 12

4. Ivy and Bean study a marine reptile with a super-long neck. It's called . . .

(Hint: *Ivy and Bean and the Ghost That Had to Go*, BOOK ❷)

a. Elasmosaur

b. Giraffopod

c. Pteranodon

d. Crocoface

5. Bean's favorite babysitter, Leona, can draw perfect . . .

(Hint: *Ivy and Bean Take Care of the Babysitter*, **BOOK ❹**)

a. goldfish

b. horses

c. wands

d. herds of sheep

6. What is Bean's middle name?

(Hint: *Ivy and Bean*, **BOOK ❶**)

a. Blue

b. Lima

c. Solon

d. Alice

7. One of the three things that Ivy flushes down the toilet belonged to Zuzu. It is a . . .

(Hint: *Ivy and Bean and the Ghost That Had to Go*, **BOOK ❷**)

a. pickle

b. sock

c. hairclip

d. worm

Beep-Beep! Math question ahead!

8. How much money does Nancy earn by babysitting Bean?

(Hint: *Ivy and Bean Take Care of the Babysitter,* BOOK ❹)

a. $20

b. $12

c. $24

d. $16

9. What's Ivy's last name?

a. McIntosh

b. Pippin

c. Braeburn

d. Smith

10. Eric tried to break the world's record for . . .

(Hint: *Ivy and Bean Break the Fossil Record,* **BOOK ❸**)

  a. eating M&Ms

  b. cartwheels

  c. longest fingernails

  d. eating scorpions

You finished—give yourself a pat on the back. Now, let's check the answer key:

1. c   2. d   3. b   4. a   5. b   6. a   7. c

8. d (She started with $20, but she had to give Bean and Ivy $4, so she ended up with $16. Get it?)

9. Ahahaha! There's no answer! Ivy's last name isn't in any of the books!

10. a

Oh boy, you're an Ivy and Bean expert now!

iVy + BEAN

BOOK 6

SNEAK PREVIEW OF BOOK 6
IVY + BEAN
DOOMED TO DANCE

It was a book that started all the trouble.

"Read, read, read! That's all grown-ups ever say to me," said Bean, "but when I finally do read, I get in trouble." She slumped in her chair. "And then the grown-ups take the book away."

Ivy nodded. "It's totally not fair," she agreed. "And they shouldn't blame us anyway. It's all Grandma's fault."

Ivy's grandma had sent her the book. It was called *The Royal Book of the Ballet.* Each chapter told the story of a different ballet, with pictures of fancy girls in feathery tutus and satin toe shoes.

Bean was at Ivy's house on the day it arrived. They were supposed to be subtracting, but they were tired of that so they ripped open the package and sat down side by side on Ivy's couch to look at *The Royal Book of the Ballet*.

"I heard that sometimes their toes bleed when they're dancing," said Bean. "The blood leaks right through the satin part."

"That's gross," said Ivy, turning the pages. Suddenly she stopped.

"Whoa, Nellie," murmured Bean, staring.

"Is she kicking his head off?" asked Ivy in a whisper.

"That's what it looks like," said Bean. "What's this one called, anyway?"

Ivy flipped back a few pages. "*Giselle*," she said, reading quickly. "It's about a girl named Giselle who, um, dances with this duke guy, but he's going to marry a princess, not Giselle, so she takes his sword and stabs herself." Ivy and Bean found the picture of that.

"Ew," said Bean. "But interesting."

"Yeah, and then she turns into a ghost with all these other girls. They're called the Wilis."

The picture showed a troop of beautiful women dressed in white. They had very long fingernails.

"And then," Ivy read on, "the duke goes to see Giselle's grave, and she comes out with the Wilis, and they decide to dance him to death." Ivy stared at the picture. "To *death.*"

Bean leaned over for a closer look. It was pretty amazing. Giselle's pointed toe had snapped the duke's head up so that his chin pointed straight up to the sky. It would fall off in a moment. The Wilis stood in a circle, waving their long fingernails admiringly.

Bean lifted the page, wishing that she could see more of the picture, but there was no more. There never was. "Wow," she said, shaking her head. "She showed him."

For a few minutes, Ivy and Bean sat in silence, thinking.

"Okay," Ivy said finally. "I'm Giselle, and you're the duke."

"All right," said Bean. "But next time, I get to be Giselle."

It was fun playing Giselle, even though Ivy's mom wouldn't let them dance with a knife and they had to use a Wiffle bat instead. After they had each been Giselle a couple of times, they were Wilis, waving long Scotch-tape fingernails as they danced various people to death.

"Mrs. Noble!" shrieked Bean. "I'm dancing Mrs. Noble to death." Ivy ran to get a pair of her mother's high heels and pretended to be Mrs. Noble, a fifth-grade teacher who had once given Ivy and Bean a lot of trouble.

Bean the Wili chased Mrs. Noble around the house, waggling her fingernails and screaming. Finally, when they were both laughing so hard they couldn't dance any more, they rushed into the kitchen and fell over on the floor.

"Well, look who's here," said Ivy's mom. She was making dinner.

"Mom," Ivy said when she got her breath back, "I *have* to take ballet class."

Ivy's mom stirred something into something else. "You had to take ice-skating, too."

Ivy wiggled her toes. "Yeah, but that was a mistake."

"How do you know ballet isn't a mistake, too? Those skates were expensive."

"Ballet is different," Ivy explained. "Ballet isn't freezing and dumb. Ballet is pretty. And it's good for you."

"I'm going to take it, too," Bean said. "That way, we can help each other during the hard parts."

Ivy's mom looked at Bean in a surprised sort of way. "You're going to take ballet?"

"Sure." Bean's mom would be happy to let her take ballet. Bean was certain of it. After all, Bean thought, her mother liked nice stuff. And ballet was nice. Except for the part where you danced people to death.

+ + + + + +

The funny thing was, Bean's mother wasn't happy to let her take ballet. Not at all.

"You'll start it, and then you'll decide you hate it and want to quit."

"No, I won't. I'll love it," Bean said.

"I'll bet you a dollar you'll hate it," said Nancy. Nancy had taken ballet when she was Bean's age. Bean remembered the time Nancy had cried because she was a chocolate bar in a ballet about candy.

"But I'm not going to be a dorky old piece of candy," Bean said. "I'm going to be a Wili." She knew better than to tell Nancy that she was going to be Giselle. Nancy would just make fun of her.

"Ha," said Nancy. "You have to be whatever they tell you to be."

"Nancy," said her mom. "I'll discuss this with Bean in private, please."

"I'll bet you, Mom," said Nancy, getting up. "I'll bet you two dollars she quits after a week."

"I'll bet you a hundred I don't," said Bean.

"Good-bye, Nancy," said their mother.

Nancy left, and Mom turned to Bean. "Now, honey, I didn't want to go into this in front of Nancy, but if I do let you take ballet, there will be no quitting."

"Quitting? Why would I quit?"

"You quit softball."

"But that was softball. All you do in softball is stand around waiting for five hundred years until it's time to hit the stupid ball. And then you miss anyway. Ballet isn't like that."

Her mother looked at her.

Bean made her eyes big. "I thought you wanted me to learn new things," she said.

Her mother looked at her some more.

"Nancy got to take ballet." Bean wiggled her lower lip. She knew that a trembling lower lip is very sad looking.

Her mother laughed. "You're drooling.

Okay. I will let you take ballet on one condition, and here it is: You will go for the whole session. Four months. Sixteen lessons. One performance. No quitting. And no complaining."

"No problem!" said Bean. She jumped up and hugged her mother. "When can I start? I already know how to kick—you want to see?